WHO EATS ORANGE?

written by Dianne White • illustrated by Robin Page

Beach Lane Books
New York   London   Toronto   Sydney   New Delhi

Who eats orange?

Bunnies in their hutches do.

Chickens in the henhouse too.

Who *else* eats orange?
Goats.

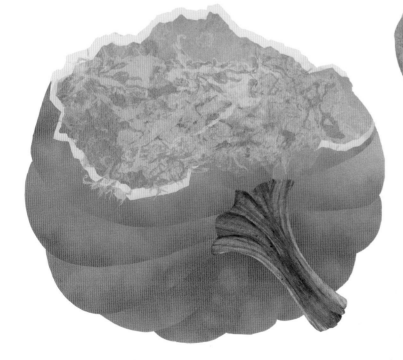

Pigs.

Gorillas too. Gorillas?
No! **Gorillas** don't eat orange.
They eat . . .

green.

Who *else* eats green?

Giraffes in savannas do.

Zebras.

Hippos.

Grunts too. Grunts?
NO! **Grunts** don't eat green.
They eat . . .

red.

Who *else* eats red?

Whales in the Pacific do.

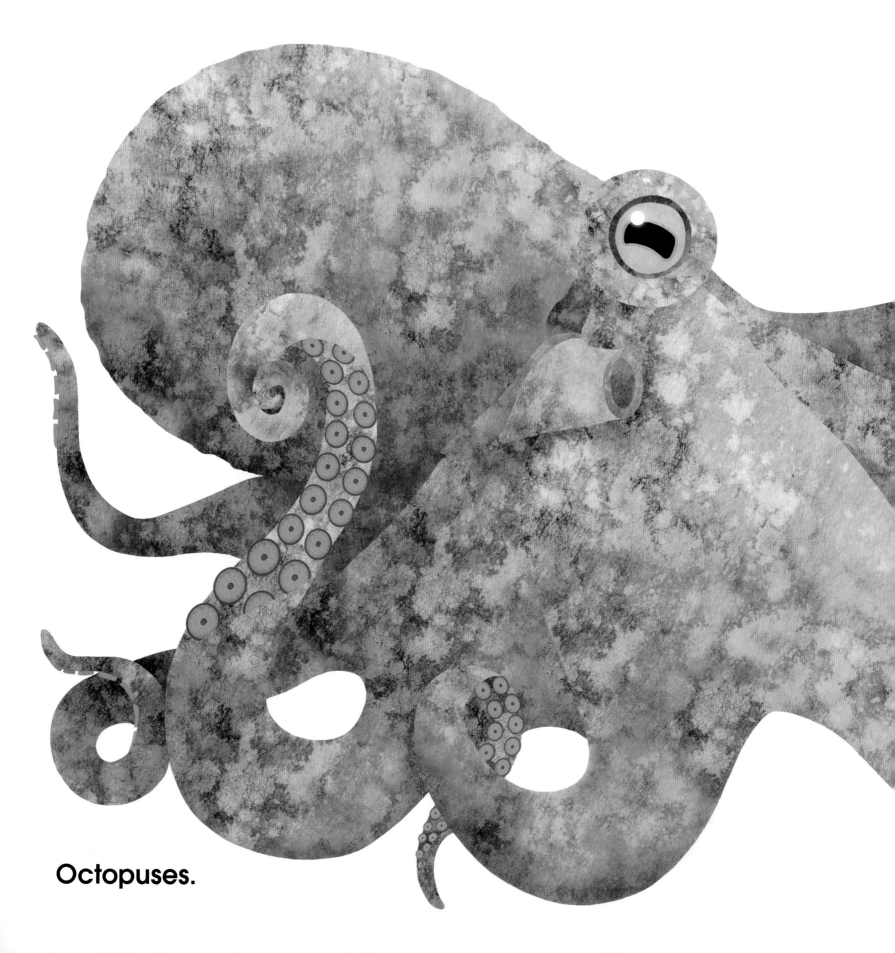

Octopuses.

Turkeys too. Turkeys?
No! **Turkeys** don't eat red.
They eat . . .

yellow.

Who *else* eats yellow?

Raccoons in the fields do.

Foxes.

Finches.

Quetzals too. Quetzals?
No! **Quetzals** don't eat yellow.
They eat . . .

purple.

Who *else* eats purple?

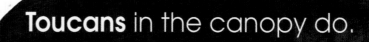

Toucans in the canopy do.

Butterflies.

Bees.

Reindeer too. Reindeer?
No! **Reindeer** don't eat purple.
They eat . . .

blue.

Who *else* eats blue?

Yellow-bellied marmots do.

Bears.

Waxwings.

Maybe you?

Why, yes, I do!

I eat a rainbow . . .

just like you.

Who eats food? Animals do. People too!

Whether a meal is harvested from a farm down the road or picked from a tree in the middle of the rain forest, all living things need food in order to live and grow.

FARM

Bunnies live in the wild but also make great pets. They are *herbivores*, which means they eat plants. Pet bunnies eat a variety of leafy green vegetables and pellets. **Carrots** and other non-leafy vegetables make a special treat.

From insects and worms to seeds and fruit, **chickens** eat almost anything! They're *omnivorous*. They like to roam, scratch at the dirt, and *forage*, or hunt, for their food. Backyard chickens enjoy all kinds of melons—including **cantaloupe**—but, like you, need a balanced diet.

Goats are *browsers*, a type of herbivore that prefers to eat leaves, twigs, vines, and shrubs. They're curious about unusual new foods and smells and are sometimes thought of as "living garbage cans." Goats have four stomachs and are considered *ruminants*—hoofed animals that chew their cuds. They love citrus, including **oranges**, and will eat both the fruit and the peel.

Pigs get their noses into everything: vegetables and fruits—such as **pumpkins**—and even bugs! Their digestive systems are adapted to opportunistic scavenging, which simply means that, much of the time, when these omnivorous animals see something on the ground, they gobble it up, and their hearty stomachs can handle it.

AFRICA

About half of the mountain **gorillas** remaining in the world live in the Virunga region of central Africa. They are *folivores*, which means they eat leaves, stems, and shoots. **Wild celery** and bamboo are favorites. In the wild, the gorilla's vegetarian diet is almost half water, so they rarely need to drink.

Giraffes are browsers that eat the leaves of bushes and trees. Their favorite is the **acacia**. Their long necks allow them to reach leaves that most animals can't. This means they don't have a lot of competition for the food they enjoy. Giraffes, like cows, don't have upper front teeth. Instead, they have a lump of tough tissue, called a *dental pad,* which allows them to tear leaves from thorny acacia branches.

Zebras are herbivorous animals that are unselective *grazers*. This means they aren't picky eaters and don't need to be! Why? It's because zebras have a very efficient digestive system that allows them to eat a variety of grasses, even those with little nutritional value. One favorite grazing grass is red grass, or **rooigras,** a green to blue-green grass that is often colored with pink and turns red with age. They also enjoy eating shrubs, herbs, twigs, leaves, and bark.

There are two species of **hippo**: the common and the pygmy hippopotamus. In the wild, they are found only in Africa. Hippos are herbivorous animals that spend much of their time near or in the water. The common hippo likes to leave the water at dusk to feed on patches of short grasses. They will occasionally eat leaves, bark, or fallen fruits. The pygmy hippo eats ferns, broad-leafed plants, and fruits, such as **mangoes**, that have fallen to the ground.

OCEAN

Blue-striped **grunts** are named for the piglike sounds they make with the help of teeth located in their throats. They forage in sea grass and mangroves, feeding on crustaceans—such as **shrimp**—clams, and small fish.

There are two main orders of **whale:** toothed and baleen. Toothed whales have teeth, perfect for catching fish or squid. Baleen whales, such as the Northern Pacific Right Whale, catch their food by filtering ocean water through fringe-like bristles made of keratin, the protein found in our fingernails and hair. Baleen whales eat a diet of **krill**, plankton, and other small marine animals.

Octopuses are *carnivores,* meat-eaters with a strong and powerful beak and eight arms to hold their prey. An octopus can taste with its skin, a highly developed sense that is possible due to the many suckers on the undersides of its arms. Octopuses eat mollusks and crustaceans, like **lobster**. Most lobsters in the ocean are a reddish- or greenish-brown color until they're caught and cooked! Then the heat breaks down proteins in the shell and only the red remains.

FOREST

Turkeys are omnivorous. In the wild, they forage for a variety of plant and animal foods and their diet changes depending on the time of year and what's available. One favorite food is the **hazelnut**. A turkey's beak is strong enough to open the shell and enjoy the tasty seed. In winter, male catkins, clusters of small flowers that hang from the branches of trees such as the American hazelnut, can be an important source of food.

Raccoons can be found just about anywhere: forests, marshes, prairies, even cities! They are omnivores, foraging in the evenings for whatever their expert hands can find—crayfish, frogs, mice, or a tasty snack from an open garbage can or a backyard garden. Families and farmers know that **corn** growing in a neighborhood garden or field may quickly become the raccoon's favorite dinner treat.

Foxes, like raccoons, are omnivores, eating both meat and vegetables. Their diet can include small animals such as rats and lizards, as well as bugs and fruit, such as **crab apples**.

The purple **finch** forages for seeds, buds, berries, and insects. It also feeds on fuzzy **catkins** of the quaking aspen. As the male catkins lengthen in early spring, their color changes from gray to pink to yellow. Eventually, the pollen sacs split, and the catkins return to gray.

RAIN FOREST

The resplendent **quetzal** (pronounced ket-SAHL) is a vibrantly colored bird considered by many to be among the most beautiful in the world. Like many birds in the rain forest, the quetzal is an omnivore. Its favorite foods are fruits of the **avocado** family. Quetzals are able to eat both the fruit and its relatively large seed. After eating, they spit out the seed, often far from where the plant grew. In this way, the quetzal helps to preserve the rain forest.

The **toucan** is one of the most well-known birds in the rain forest. Like the quetzal,

toucans are omnivores. They use their colorful bills, the largest in the bird class, to pick up small fruits, like the **acai berry**, which ripens to a dark purple color. They are playful eaters and sometimes pick up berries with the tip of their bill and toss them up in the air before catching them in their mouths.

The cloudless sulphur **butterfly** feeds on nectar from many different plants. One of these is the **morning glory**, whose trumpet-shaped flower comes in a variety of colors, including purple.

The carpenter **bee** is large with a shiny black abdomen. It feeds on the sweet nectar of its favorite flowers, including the **passionflower,** a climbing vine with edible fruit and flowers of different colors. The carpenter bee's size and foraging behavior make it an efficient pollinator.

TUNDRA

In the cold months of winter, when food is scarce, **reindeer** in the tundra survive on **lichen** called "reindeer moss." Lichen is the result of an unusual partnership between a fungus and a blue-green alga called cyanobacteria. It grows on the ground and is usually a pale gray-blue or gray-green color.

Yellow-bellied marmots are generally herbivores that like to feed on the leaves and blossoms of a variety of grasses and forbs, such as **alpine forget-me-nots**, which are some of the first flowers to bloom on the tundra. They also eat fruit, grains, and sometimes bugs.

Black **bears** are powerful omnivorous mammals that can have black, brown, white, or even bluish fur. Their diet includes plants

and fruits like **saskatoon berries**, which, though similar in appearance to blueberries, are more closely related to the apple family.

Cedar **waxwings** love the sweet taste of blue honeysuckles, also called **haskap**. They're one of a small number of North American birds that can survive on a fruit-only diet for several months at a time. The cedar waxwing is different from many other fruit-eating birds because it doesn't remove the seeds and spit them up. Instead, the seeds pass through its system undigested.

AROUND THE WORLD

Humans eat a rainbow of different foods. This isn't just tasty—it's important for our health! For example, **oranges** are rich in vitamin C. **Acai berries** are packed with antioxidants. And **carrots** and **cantaloupe** are excellent sources of vitamin A, which we need for healthy eyes. Filling our bodies with a wide variety of colorful fruits and vegetables ensures that we get enough of the important vitamins, nutrients, and fiber that we need— just like all the creatures in this book.

For my grandson, Kale,
who fills my days with color and light
—D. W.

For Steve Jenkins
—R. P.

BEACH LANE BOOKS

An imprint of Simon & Schuster Children's Publishing Division
1230 Avenue of the Americas, New York, New York 10020
Text copyright © 2018 by Dianne White
Illustrations copyright © 2018 by Robin Page

For information about special discounts for bulk purchases, please contact Simon & Schuster Special
Sales at 1-866-506-1949 or business@simonandschuster.com.
The Simon & Schuster Speakers Bureau can bring authors to your live event.
For more information or to book an event, contact the Simon & Schuster Speakers Bureau at
1-866-248-3049 or visit our website at www.simonspeakers.com.

Book design by Robin Page
The text for this book was set in ITC Avant Garde Gothic.
The illustrations for this book were rendered in Adobe Photoshop.

Manufactured in China
0518 SCP
First Edition
2 4 6 8 10 9 7 5 3 1
Library of Congress Cataloging-in-Publication Data
Names: White, Dianne, author. | Page, Robin, 1957– illustrator.
Title: Who eats orange? / Dianne White ; illustrated by Robin Page.
Description: First edition. | New York : Beach Lane Books, (2018) | Audience: Ages 0–8. |
Audience: K to grade 3. | Includes bibliographical references and index.
Identifiers: LCCN 2017042656 | ISBN 9781534404083 (hardcover : alk. paper)
| ISBN 9781534404090 (eBook)
Subjects: LCSH: Animals—Food—Juvenile literature. | Food habits—Juvenile literature. |
Color of food—Juvenile literature.
Classification: LCC QL756.5.W45 2018 | DDC 591.5—dc23 LC record available at
https://lccn.loc.gov/2017042656